ISBN: 978-1-7332672-6-7 (paperback)

eBook available for immediate download (free on Amazon with
kindle unlimited plan)

Moore Substance Publishing
Original publication 2020

Edited by Marilyn Beach

Table of Contents

Capítulo Uno (Side Funeral)

Sounds from the musicians' instruments filled the sanctuary, signifying the conclusion of the preacher's eulogy. Melanie hadn't heard but maybe a word or two of it. Her thoughts had been circulating like money at a crap game. After looking for ANY reason not to go, she finally broke down and resolved to show her respect for the love of her life. Fortunately, she found a space in the back of the church next to her bae's best friend Dillion McDaniel. Her heart, Young Will, and his roll dawg Dillion were closer than cleavage in a Victoria Secret's push-up bra. They were known around the city as "Wheeling and Dealing." So of course, with Melanie being enamored with Willis, she was cool with D-Mc as well.

"How you holding up?" Dillion asked. Melanie just shook her head. She felt that if she had answered truthfully, she would have lost it and the tears would've streamed like Netflix.

"You?" she inquired.

"I'm still in shock. How I'm spose to get ova dis one?" he rhetorically asked. "I'm neva gettin ova dis!" he emphatically added. His death would be as equally taxing on Mel. Over the past year, she and Willis had a covalent type bond. He had really opened up to her over that time. They had been to Destin, Florida, for Thanksgiving, spent New Year's Eve in Las Vegas, and even enjoyed an amazingly uninterrupted Father's

Day BBQ together. They'd actually had more meaningful moments as one, than he and his actual girlfriend had.

"Look at her up there like she's part of the family," Mel sarcastically pointed out.

"I know right," Dillion concurred. "She always liked the spotlight and attention," he added.

"That should be me up there," Melanie thought to herself. Had it been a year or two later, it may have possibly been her sitting up front with his family. But since he had a girlfriend that'd been tried, tested and approved by the family, she got first dibs over the up-and-coming love interest. Not to mention they were still coinhabiting in a house they'd bought, so Mel was delegated to the best kept secret. He was going to wait until one of them moved out or they sold the house to bring Melanie to the forefront. It seemed simpler that way. "What she keep looking back here pointing for?!" Mel internally asked herself. "She must know something. I don't have time to play. It is what it is if she's feeling frisky. I'll drag her in between these pews if she says something out of line. Today is NOT the day. And I BEEN ready to let off some steam," she continued to think. "Or maybe she doesn't and I'm just tripping off that blunt from this morning. Either way it's whatever," she resolved in her mind.

D-Mc interrupted her thoughts with a statement, "Welp, it's almost dat time. They collecting dem flowers. Still don't seem real."

Mel turned and whispered to D-Mc, "The only plant he ever cared about was Mary Jane." They laughed in a manner to not turn the heads of anyone else and gave one another that "OK!" look. As the procession of family and friends tailed the casket to the exit, Mel grew more and more anxious to get out of there and go home. As fate would have it, the line paused just long enough where Willis' girlfriend was right next to the row that Mel and D-Mc were on.

She looked past D-Mc and asked Melanie, "You're coming to the repast, right? I know y'all were close and I'd love for all his real friends to be there. I'm sure it'd mean a lot to him."

"It'd mean a lot to me, if you got outta my face and kept walking," Mel reckoned inwardly. "You think I'm stupid, hoe?! I'm not bout to let you and yo jackal friends jump me, then I have to come back and kill ALL y'all. Nawl, I'm good, chick," Mel further thought. "We'll see," she replied. "You have the address, right?" She turned and asked D-Mc.

"No doubt," he confirmed.

Willis' woman by title, glanced at Dillion, gave a subtle eye-roll, looked back at Mel and said, "Cool, looking forward to it."

"I bet you are," Mel internalized, I bet... you... are.

Capítulo Dos (Today was a good day)

"I will not let ANYTHING make me mad, lose my temper, cuss, or get into physical altercations. Today will be a GOOD day," Lawrence repeated. Sheryl had been on him about his attitude, irritability and lack of patience. She'd been sending him YouTube videos, articles, social media posts, books, and encouraging him to proclaim things aloud, like the phrase she'd just had him recite. He was giving as much effort as possible and being a good sport about it. He really did want to be happier and less agitated on a daily basis with those around him. Plus, he thought it might help with his relationship with Sheryl, who with all the constant dictatorial support (as much as she meant well), had become rather vexing herself. Metaphorically speaking, he was one foot and two hands out the door already. "Thank you, love, I appreciate your effort, patience and all the ways you help me grow," Lawrence uttered. He'd picked up a few talking tips from the latest self-help book that Sheryl had politely pressured him to read, on how to communicate more effectively. But honestly, he was anxious to start his day and have some personal time away from Taskmaster Tammy. He'd given her that nickname, unbeknownst to her of course. "Alright, I'm going to get my haircut, I'll be back later," Lawrence said, as he tried to promptly ease out the door.

"Wait!" Sheryl hastily yelled from the bathroom. Can you bring me back some washing liquid, so I can wash some clothes while you're gone?"

Lawrence instantly thought, "It's ALWAYS something with her. Why can't she go get it? What's she got planned besides reality shows, Shade Room gossip and ordering take out?" On Saturdays, barber shops are known to be crowed like the Chandni Chowk market in Old Delhi, so it's best to get there as early as possible. He had purposely gone to bed early, in hopes of beating most of the other patrons there. He took a deep breath and answered, "Of course I can, I'm just going to get a haircut. No big deal."

"Thank you, sweetie, you're the best," Sheryl replied. Lawrence headed out and made a beeline to the closest store. He hopped out the ride on a mission, with two things in mind, get the Tide then Roll, like a dyslexic Alabama fan. He got to the door and realized he didn't have his mask. He quickly pivoted and spun around like Hakeem Olajuwon in his prime, then jogged back to his vehicle. He frantically searched for his mask that was always in the side of his door. After he failed to find it, he began to blame Sheryl for moving it. After all, she was the only other person who had access to his vehicle. But why on EARTH would she have moved it? Before any ill thoughts permeated his mental about Sheryl, he noticed a young man selling masks out the corner of his eyes. "AH HA!!" he exclaimed, "Just what the doctor ordered." He paid the ten dollars, which he thought was way too high for a flimsy, cheaply designed cotton mask, but understood the concept of supply and demand, then went in the store.

Upon his victorious return from purchasing the detergent, while avoiding talking to anyone, he noticed a dent in his vehicle. He immediately looked in the sky with a "why me" countenance. It was a classic hit-and-run, without a note attached. No name, number or insurance information, leaving him to file the claim on his own and take the time out to get it fixed. He sat in his car, took a deep breath, then proceeded to go drop off the detergent, so he could go to the shop. Before he even made it to the stop light, his tire light started flashing like Gordon. He got out and noticed that his driver's side tire was losing air at a rapid rate. His spirit was beginning to deflate at a similar pace. He closed his eyes, put his head in his right hand and sighed bitterly. After changing the tire, he made it home, sat the Tide on the inside of the door, texted Sheryl and ran back to his vehicle, so that she couldn't verbally utter another request. At this point, he figured he should grab something to eat, so that he'd have the strength to endure the wait he was inevitably going to have at the barber shop. He ordered a combo from a fast food establishment, in route to the urban tonsorial parlor. After trading salutations with the other brethren in the shop, he found a peaceful spot to enjoy his meal, while he waited. Sadly, his plan of enjoying a tasty meal, was foiled when he saw that they'd left the meat out of his deluxe burger. There was cheese, lettuce, pickles, onions, tomatoes, dressing and bacon, but no patty to be found. He looked up, gave a grin that summarized his day and ate his fries.

When he finally got in the chair, he felt somewhat of a relief, as if, for the moment, everything would be alright. The barbershop, particularly when it's their turn to get taken care of, can be a rest haven for men. It's a therapeutic sanctuary for even the most savage being. It was as pleasant as usual, until, "AHHH," Lawrence yelled.

"My bad, bruh," his barber apologized. He had inadvertently nicked the side of Lawrence's ear. Lawrence began to spew blood like a hemophiliac from Bompton. After his ear was successfully bandaged, and his haircut finalized, he decided to go straight home, not pass go, and not collect two hundred dollars.

Peering in the rearview mirror on his way home, Lawrence began to talk to himself, "This is what Holyfield must've felt like after the Tyson fight." "What a day, what a day," he concluded.

When he got home, Sheryl asked, with a smile that could light up the darkest valley during midnight, "How was your day?!"

"It...it was a good day," Lawrence responded.

"SEE! I told you if you just kept claiming it and applying those things in the books, that things would be different for you," she confidently retorted.

"Yep, you called it," he agreed in speech, as he masked his facial expression like an N95 covering.

"AND to make your day even better, I have some great news that I found out this morning," she happily added.

"You're moving out?" he thought, before he asked, "What is it?"

Her smile grew bigger than the Michellin Man as she revealed, "I'm expecting!!! I took a pregnancy test when you were getting ready to leave this morning..." She continued to share her joy, but all he heard was the *Curb Your Enthusiasm* theme song playing.

Capítulo Tres (Common Mistake?)

The downpour was abrupt and unexpected, like a woman's water breaking, who was blindly unaware of her pregnancy. The evening atmosphere had seemingly changed from "Classical skies" to the "Dark ages" in a historical fashion. The consistent bodybuilders, lukewarm guest and gym unicorns alike, were amazed and talked about the sudden weather transformation.

"The ONE day out of the month, I decide to come to the gym...THIS happens," Trisha said, as she stared out of the window, mouth half open, in a state of disbelief. La'Tavious couldn't contain his laughter. Trisha turned and said, "Real funny huh. Everything's a joke to Mr. La La Laughs, ain't it."

He tried to compose himself before replying, "I mean, even you have to admit that it's hilariously ironic. No? Not even a little? Gone let that smile out, frowning won't stop the rain."

The tension in her jaws, eased up slightly as she spoke, "Boy, I'm not bout to mess with you OR this rain. And I'm definitely not messing up my hair for the week! Ion care if I have to spend da night in dis sweat museum, I am NOT going out in that rain." No one in the gym had an umbrella or poncho.

Back laughing again, he offered a solution, "Don't trip, I have an umbrella in my ride, I'll just run out and grab it for you. I'll be right back." Fortunately, it was early fall and La'Tavious had worn his favorite hoody with his Jordan shorts. His brother had given it to him, before he deployed last summer. Trisha walked with him to the door, as they continued to engage in small talk. He flipped the top of the hood on his head and jetted to the parking lot. The few flickering, faulty lights that still worked, were overwhelmed and essentially rendered ineffective due to the daunting darkness. The rainfall was so intense that you couldn't distinguish the direction of the turbulent winds or which way to turn your face to prevent from being pelted into temporary blindness. La'Tavious brilliantly balanced his way through it all, like a seasoned captain aboard a stormy ship, on his way safely to his destination.

Meanwhile, in an adjacently parked vehicle, John was making a suggestion, "Have you considered going to your immediate supervisor about it first?" John and Karen had been sitting in her vehicle, discussing some issues that she had with several co-workers, while waiting the storm out. She was hell-bent on going straight to the top.

"No!" she passionately replied, "Because Sabrina never does anything! She just says that she's going to look further into it, and nothing ever happens. I'm sick of IT!" John continued reasoning with her until she interrupted his logical argument, screaming out, "OH MY GOSH, someone is breaking into your ride!!"

John's neck snapped to the direction of his ride and replied, "Wait here!" as he opened the door and accelerated around the rear of her vehicle. La'Tavious was still struggling to open the door. John shouted, "You picked the wrong ride today

BUDDY" and pulled out his concealed weapon. La'Tavious was oblivious to what John was doing and yelling. His only concern was getting into his vehicle and out of the storm. As the lightening rippled across the black horizon and the thunder roared like a ferocious lion, bullets pierced through the hoody and flesh of La'Tavious. Trisha, still looking out the window, was veritably stunned, while Karen was stupefied.

Trished bellowed, "Somebody call the police!!!" as she dashed out the doorway. Karen, who was nestled safe and dry inside her ride, had already called 911 and was talking to dispatch. She made the call, as soon as John jumped out her sedan. John was standing over La'Tavious' body. John's emotions of unbridled rage were subsiding and being replaced with remorse and mortification. His wrath was fueled by the fact that his car had been broken into twice over the last three months, and one of his friends was robbed downtown within that same time span. Those events had ultimately led to him getting a pistol and concealed handgun permit. He reflected on those incidents daily and longed to catch the next person breaking into his ride, so he could exact immediate judgment and teach them a lesson, as if he were the professor of punishment. Regrettably, he didn't feel like an instructor but more like a student who failed miserably.

As Trisha kneeled over La'Travious' motionless body, she verbally assaulted John with obscenities reserved for the disgustfully wretched. The police were unable to initially sort things out. Karen repeatedly explicated the account of John's car being broken into while Trisha madly explained that the murderer had shot La'Travious before he could get into his ride and bring back an umbrella. John was mummified and mute. One of the officers picked up the key fob that was between La'Travious's body and the ride. When he hit the button to unlock the doors, lights began to beam intermittently two rows over. It was the same color and model vehicle. It even had the same tint as the one he lay next to.

Capítulo Cuatro (Move, I'm on a mission)

"Yeah, you're right," Kelly replied, "I should probably get going. But then again, what they gonna do, fire me?" After the joint laughter subsided, she continued, "But nawl, that's true. Plus, you know how this morning traffic be. People driving like they ain't got no sense. I'll call you later on today, boo." Kelly ended the call, double checked the time, then continued to get dressed. At this point, it'd take a miracle for her be on time. Not that she was overly concerned with it. "Welp, it's donut time," she said to herself, as she strolled out the door and down the steps. She learned a long time ago, if you're going to be late, the least you can do is bring the crew doughnuts. She pulled into the shopping center where the "Yum Yum Donut" shop was. "Great! Jussssssst Great. Everyone and their grandma here today," she said while shaking her head, "What, these people don't have food at home? Now I'm a definitely be late." She got in line and perused her favorite social media sites.

"Ten dolla and thirty-five cent," the cashier repeated, as she attempted to get Kelly's attention.

Kelly looked up from her phone, gave her eleven dollars and said with assurance, "You know what, keep the change. I need a blessing in my life anyway." She grabbed the box of pastries, cup of java, pocketed a handful of napkins and moseyed on out the door. "Alright, it's GO time." She pumped and propped herself up for the drive, then threw on some

Young Jeezy for her inner thug motivation. On the highway, she weaved in and out of traffic like she was riding a motorbike, mashing her horn anytime someone slowed her progress or yelled "Come on pee-pullllllllll, act like you've driven before." Other times she loudly uttered, "Move, I'm on a mission." Kelly even shared the center finger with a driver or two, who wouldn't get over in a timely manner, further contributing to her tardiness. She was, however, humble enough to give an apology when she cut someone off, "Sorry...I'm on a mission," or not as modest when she'd say, "Calm down, you act like I hit you," as she continued to zoom like an online meeting.

As Kelly neared the parking area she preferred, she frowned and complained, "What are all these people doing here so early?! I can't even get a good spot." She continued to murmur her discontent, as she lowered the music and pulled into a parking space, "We need to have our own section, separate from the visitors. They can't expect us to cheerfully smile, after walking a mile." She put the ride in park and added a minor pep to her step. Not that she was genuinely in a rush, but she wanted to avoid as many people as possible who knew her name, that she couldn't remember. She claimed to have never been good at remembering names, cringing on the inside when they used hers, and she couldn't reciprocate that personal greeting. Upon seeing Ms. Shirley, she perked up, "Sorry I'm late, but I come bearing gifts!"

"I told Kevin you'd be here and not to worry," Ms. Shirley kindly replied. "We had Joshua cover your section until you got here. If you're ever running late again," they'd actually be surprised if she was ever on time, "just text or call one of us, so we know." That was a nice way of reminding Kelly what she'd already been asked to do several times in the past. She was habitually late and never let anyone know. I guess at that point, it'd become understood.

Kelly responded, "Yes ma'am, I will. I'm a go and a relieve Joshua now. Hope to see you later; if not, have a blessed day." Instead of doing just that, she went into the bathroom, fixed her hair, made a phone call, and finished the rest of her coffee. When she finally came around the corner where Joshua was, she readied her contrite facial expression and meekly said, "I am soooooo sorry. The director pulled me aside and was seeing if I could assist in some other areas next month. I didn't want to be rude and cut her short, but I was thinking about you the entire time. Ms. Shirley mentioned that you were the one covering my spot. I appreciate you more than you know."

"It's never a problem to fill in; I love what I do," Joshua replied. "Well, it's all yours now; if I don't see you later, have a blessed week."

"You too!" Kelly replied. Then she turned and greeted the first few people walking up, "Welcome to Mega Ministries, we're glad you chose to join us for worship today. If this is your first time, or you haven't in the past, please fill out a visitor's card, so that we can learn more about you, share important information, and give you an opportunity to briefly meet with Pastor after service." After about five minutes of greeting, her internal thoughts had totally consumed her focus and she was ready to sit down. "Why are they coming in this entrance and why are they so late? Church started 10 minutes ago. I swear, some people just don't care." As time neared for her to retire for the morning and join the congregation, she was mindful to take care of one more task. She spoke into her watch "Hey Siri, remind me to take eleven dollars off my tithes."

Capítulo Cinco (Unapproved Buggage)

"Now boarding rows five through six for flight 2245 to Atlanta."
Charles continued watching the game on the screen in the
airport lobby. He was never one to rush to wait. He could care
less if he was the last person to board the plane, since they
were leaving at the same time and seats already assigned.
When they called the last set of passengers, he grabbed his
carry on, put his bookbag over his right shoulder and headed to
the line. He looked ahead at the passengers in front of him.
*Her bag's definitely not a carryon. Heck, if I knew they let people
bring that size bag on the plane, I wouldn't have paid for my
luggage. But then again, it'd be my luck that if I bring that exact
same size bag as my carryon, they'll try to make me pay on the
spot. I'm a be like Chris Rock in "I'm Gonna Git You Sucka"
though, 'How much for one sock? I can't afford to pay for
everything to fly. What if I just hold a few items in my hand?'*
Charles noticed the boarding agent. *She kinda nice. I wonder
what that mouth look like under the mask though. I mean her
shape is above par and from nose to forehead she's doable. But
I hate a tacky weave. Look like she got that hair from the store
and slapped in right on her head. Terrible. Hopefully someone
puts her up on game. It's a shame to be built like 'Yes Please'
with hair like 'No thank you.'*
He shook his head, then looked back at the people checking in.
Couldn't be me, not today. Everybody putting their phones on

the scanner to check in, then right back to their face. They gone be wondering how they caught Covid. Ain't no telling who all sneezed, coughed, spit and everything else on their phone, then put theirs on the scanner before them. They'll be playing on their phone while eating food without hand sanitizer now, then later, be mad that the mask didn't work. After he handed his printed boarding pass to the gate agent, he made his way to the plane, stored his small carryon in the overhead bin and found his seat. He was tall, so it was always a plus to have an aisle seat. That way he could at least fully stretch one of his legs out during the flight. Once the flight was cruising at a comfortable altitude, he started surveying the scene.

I wonder what that baby's thinking right now. If it even realizes we're thirty plus thousand feet in the sky. Awwww look at the couple. They look so happy together. She leaning on his shoulder while he kissing her head. This probably their first trip together. Be funny, on the way back, they can't stand each other. It's a thin line between puppy love and doggy disgust. He analyzed a few more passengers then noticed something small and brownish moving 4 rows up on the right near the overhead bins. He couldn't tell if it was a spider, beetle, oversized mite, or some new species of insect. It was 2020, so you never know. He looked around to see if anyone else saw it. *I know I'm not the only one seeing this. Can't' be. What is that? How'd it even get here. I've never seen a bug on a plane. I thought they were cleaning even better due to Covid. Did it come in someone's bag or purse? What if it gets into someone's carryon in the storage? Then when they get to their hotel or home, it bites them or is pregnant and starts populating. Are there more of them or is this the Lone Ranger of killer insects? Somebody needs to do something. If it was me, I would want someone to warn me. I would, but, nawl, you never know how people will react nowadays. What if I go to warn her then it disappears or crawls in the bin and she think I'm just trying to be fresh? What do I do?* He continued to mull over the scenario and hoped that someone else would speak up. Charles wasn't shy but he never knew how to approach a stranger to point something out, such as their hair being messed up, clothes on backwards, stain on a garment, food in their teeth, or smudge on their face. Some people are stouthearted when it comes to things like that, but Charles wasn't one of them. He typically assumed the worst response would ensue, until deciding to look away and hope for the best. The best wasn't playing out this time though. With his eyes fixed on the unknown creature, it suddenly dropped from overhead and into the passenger's hair. He was taken aback as if it had landed on himself.

She didn't feel that? I wonder if she's ever going to feel it. What if it starts living in there and colonizes? They say we eat bugs all the time while sleeping. Not sure how true that is, but a lot of people say it. I once read that the average human consumes at least a pound of insects, flies, maggots, spiders and other bugs a year in their sleep, but then again, how trustworthy is everything on the internet?

His rabbit-hole thoughts were interrupted as she slapped the back of her head and looked around to see if someone was messing with her. He quickly looked away and got back to his thoughts.

Yep! Knew it wouldn't be long before she felt something. It had to have bitten her. What if she dies? What if she lives but starts some new disease, like West Nile-Covid 2-Malaria-Lime 11? His thoughts then switched from a new world pandemic to personal concerns. *What if another one is on ME?* He readjusted his body, then moved his hands over his head, neck and other uncovered body parts, as inconspicuously as possible. *What if it's in my shoes or resting in my socks and I awaken it when I start to walk? What if it's in my carryon, defecating over all my belongings? Please don't let it violate my toothbrush.* Needless to say, he was on edge the rest of the flight. It's funny how something so small or potentially insignificant, can have such a grand impact on our thoughts, mood and emotions.

Capítulo Seis (Did she really say that?)

"Eeeeeee," Devin projected his voice as loud as possible towards Everette's window.

Everette stuck his head halfway out the window and yelled back, "Come upstairs, the doors unlocked," then went back to getting ready. Devin flung open the room door about forty seconds later.

"Yo! Why it take you foreva and a day to get ready? I texted you ova an hour ago. We juss gone ball E. You act like the hoods next top model gone see and recruit you."

"Listennnnn mannnn," Everette, still looking in the mirror, replied, "everyone wasn't blessed with the gift of stunningness. You got your talents and I got mine. Don't block my shine homie."

"Your shine???" Devin questioned, "Scratch all dat; you blocking the MONEY. And the money's what's gone really help you shine, playboy. The two of them would catch the bus to the Northern Hills on the weekend and play the affluent kids for their spare change. It was nothing for those rich kids to "lose" some spare change, especially to a local legend like Devin Lewis. He was the five-star basketball, all state, all world athlete that everyone adored. The wealthy kids were basically paying for his entertainment. They had no real shot, pardon the pun, at even beating Devin in a one-on-two game, much less a two-on-two match-up. He just needed someone to pass him the ball and look good. His childhood friend since pre-K, Everette Stewart was more than happy to fulfill that role. E was slightly better than the adolescents from Northern Hills, which wasn't even good enough to make the squad that Devin had led to the state championship last year. They two were seniors now. One was heavily recruited by the top colleges in the nation, while the other was highly sought after by the young ladies. They were mesmerized by E's hair, eyes, skin tone and swag. You'd be hard-pressed to find more than a dozen of young tenders at their school, who hadn't considered what a child with him would look like.

"Money???" E's tone and facial expression, were one of 'How DARE you.' "You mean like dis?" He pulled out a wad of cash, accompanied by a 'Don't disrespect me like that' demeanor.

"NICCAU," Devin leaped up from where he was sitting, "Where da fuq you get dat stack from?!" E erupted with laughter. He tried to keep a straight face but lost all composure when he saw the shocked look that Devin displayed.

"Dis is two months' of rent money my boi," E explained. "Moms left it on da counter befoe she dipped to work dis morning. Landlord s'pose to scoop it up later or Monday. I couldn't pass up da chance to stunt for the gram, ya know."

"E," Devin grabbed him by both shoulders and looked him in the depths of his soul, "listen to me. I real deal dreamed about dis last night. We had money to blow n every thang to show."

Devin backed out of his grasp and made a statement, "It's too early to be pop'n pills kid. You must be high from last night, if you think I'm STUPID enough to take my own moms rent money."

"E!!" punching his right hand inside his own left palm, "you not listening." He grabbed E by his shoulders again then continued, "We're not stealing, we're investing it. Think about it, the only reason we don't get moe paper, is cuz we don't have enough to bet big. THIS is our chance to hit a lick then split," he pointed to the rent money. "We ain't neva EVA lost and we won't start today. I can beat dem boys blind wit one arm behind my back while tweeting." Honestly, he probably could have. That's just how trash they were, and E knew it. Devin could tell he was considering it, so he added, "Dem J's coming out, the PS5 bout to drop, you ALWAYS eyeing fresh fits, and you KNOW you gonna wanna buy all yo hoes something legit for Christmas." Facts upon facts. E had heard no lies and he DID want that PS5. His mom was working seven days a week, just to stay afloat and he hadn't talked to his deadbeat dad since grade school, so it wasn't like he had other financial resources or options.

"My mom said da landlord already be letting us pay late, if we don't pay dis month, we gone be sleeping under a bridge," E countered.

"Did she really say that?" Devin asked. E couldn't stop thinking about everything he wanted and could now have.

"Aiight, but we gotta hurry. Don't be clowning or phuckin round wit dem buckets today," E demanded. "I ain't tryna hear her mouf, if he comes and da money ain't on dat counter."

When they entered the park at Northern Hills, they could barely contain their exuberance. They'd texted on the way, explaining they couldn't stay all day, so instead of playing a bunch of games for forty dollars a pop, they'd only come if they could play one game for the whole kit and caboodle. The residents were to combine their money, pick their two best "stars" and would even be spotted 8 points going to 15. Everette's two months' rent was leisure day at the mall for any of the residents there. So, combining their money was like pitching in to buy a six pack and enjoying a game for the average American. Devin and E started down zero to eight and easily lead 12 to 9 after a short time. It was lightwork for Devin. For the 13th point, he put his helpless defender in a blender, blew by him and reverse dunked it. The way the bystanders jumped and cheered, you'd have thought they had their money on the winning team. You would've also assumed that E had a heart attack the way he grabbed his chest and couldn't breathe after Devin landed wrong and seriously twisted his ankle. After it was obvious that he couldn't finish the game (no matter how much E begged and pleaded) and the locals weren't going to allow them to postpone or cancel the bet, Everette was regulated to picking a replacement and leading the unlikely duo. In a normal situation, up 4 with 2 to go, against relatively lower talent, he would've sealed the deal. But it proved to be much too much pressure, with all that was on the line. And the other team had gained more confidence than a man shooting at a caged lion. As the final shot of his opponents dropped through the pearly mesh, E collapsed. He'd never felt such pain and hopelessness before. He'd went from counting his blessings to come to calculating the hours he had to live.

Ch. 7 (Ernest Hemingway challenge)

Wanted: American equality, serious solutions only.

Capítulo Ocho (Shoeshine)

Duke and Todd were having a conversation as if William was invisible. It'd been a typical conversation about life after the war and what the future for of America was. And by America they meant the whites. They didn't respect the Negro very much. Blacks were a fourth-class citizen in their eyes. On their totem pole, it was: Successful whites, middle class whites, lower class whites, then Negros. They'd shared their perspective with one another on several topics, from coloreds serving in the military, segregation, jobs, Jackie Robinson signing with the Brooklyn Dodgers and UFO sightings.

"Make sure to put a good shine on em," Duke directed William, "I have an important meeting later on this evening."

"Yes sir," William replied without looking up. As a part time boot shiner, he was privy to all types of conversations, thoughts and philosophies. Some were beneficial and others meaninglessly ignorant. It was rare that any of them triggered negative emotions, and this one was no different. The nonsense went in one ear and out the other.

"A colored man shouldn't be in a position to lead white troops or make major decisions," Todd responded to Duke, "That's just too much pressure for their intellect." He looked down at William and added, "No disrespect but history and science just prove that we're better leaders."

Still diligently shining shoes, William waived his righthand up at Todd, "None taken, sir, I understand." William was a true professional, courteous and rarely lost his bearing. He'd actually served in the war that the other two only pontificated about. From 1942 until the war ended, he valiantly contributed to his country. He, along with many other African Americans, were disappointed but not dumbfounded, to return home and still be treated as and considered less. Even the employment opportunities were less than desirable and available, for some of the same jobs they'd mastered and performed overseas.

"If they'd just learn a skill, they'd be hired like the next man," Duke assured all who could hear. "You can't be lazy in America and think you can get ahead." Ironically, there was a hint of truth in his statement. His parents had provided the best schools, financial support and even reliable contacts, but due to his slothfulness he'd actually gone backwards and squandered the head start he was afforded in life. William, on the other hand, was an industrious gentleman who'd acquired some impressive skills prior to and during his enlisted time.

"There we go," William finished an excellent polish and stood up, "Thank you both for your business and I hope I can be of some of service to you both, in the future."

Duke glanced at his shoes, then back at William and nodded his head up in down, "Not bad, not bad at all son." His facial expression revealed just how impressed he was at the great job. He paid the exact price then explained, "I don't have any money for a tip, but I can give ya some advice that'll help your life."

"I'd appreciate that," William facetiously replied.

"Work hard, be grateful, save up and one day you might able to afford some nice things."

By the looks of it, and not just when he buffed boots, you wouldn't have guessed the type of financial position that William was in. His parents owned two successful businesses in Greenwood before they were destroyed during the hideous Wall Street massacre of 1921. He'd chosen to fly under the radar and keep a low profile due to that historically tragic event. He owned land and a prominent mechanic shop in the town. The locals assumed it was owned by a Caucasian and that he was simply one of the workers, but he was, indeed, the head honcho. He'd worked on trucks, hummers, planes, tanks, choppers, and more while in the military. He was a natural born handyman that honed his skills while abroad. His time in the war also helped shape his demeanor, speech, and mindset, while he learned to keep his enemies close, as they revealed their true heart and strategies.

"Thank you for sharing those words of wisdom, sir," he replied to Duke. "I'll be sure to keep em close to my heart now," he sarcastically ended the conversation, then turned and gently greeted the next customer.

Capítulo Nueve (You got it)

"It's always great when the late game doesn't disappoint," the commentator said.

"You ain't neva lied," Deante agreed with the analyst on his tv screen. He reached for the remote and hit the guide button to see if he could find anything interesting on for his viewing nightcap. He was off the next day and was planning on sleeping in until lunch, possibly even dinner time. He'd been working tirelessly on the job. Before he could find something suitable to watch, he heard, "And now, for the postgame report."

"SHOOT!!" He dropped the remote, put his drink down and slapped the sofa, "I FORGOT to email that report. I KNEW I shoulda did it Friday." Friday, he wanted to leave as early as possible, rationalizing: he had plenty of time over the weekend. Technically he did, but practically he failed to take advantage of it, and now it was a few hours before midnight. He went to his truck and got the work laptop out. The flash drive still in the USB port. He powered it on, rubbed his hands together and said, "Allllright, let me send this file out an we good."

Ten minutes later and things were not good. "Why is this thing not connecting to the WiFi?!" He grew more and more frustrated. He was far from Tech savvy. He just knew that it had worked, since his ex-girlfriend hooked it up for him two months ago. It was too late to try calling her now, especially since she had a new man. He wasn't trying to intrude, just in case they were together. After staring at the wall until it appeared blurry, and bouncing rejected ideas across his frontal lobe, he decided to call the internet company. "They claim to have round the clock support, well we gone find out tonight."

"We're currently experiencing a high volume of calls, your wait time is approximately 14 minutes," the automated voice recording relayed the message.

"FOURTEEN minutes?" his face balled up. "High volume of calls?" He questioned, "Who's calling at this time of night on a Sunday? They need to stop."

Then he heard, "If you're calling about internet service, there's an outage in your area. We are currently working on the problem. It should be resolved within the next 4 to 12 hours." He hung up and threw his cell phone at the foot of the bed. He exhaled wearily.

"I haven't had this position for a full month yet and I'm already slipping. I had ONE job this weekend," he internalized as he smirked and shook his head. He was punctual, dependable, efficient and honest. However, he did lie about being "good with computers" when they were looking to fill a vacant supervisor's role. His ex-boo was the one who had done or walked him through everything computer related, up until their split. The company didn't know that though. They were none the wiser and he'd given them no reason to question or doubt. Suddenly he had a sensible idea. "I'll just drive to her place. Her internet should be on." At that point, he didn't know what else to do. He figured he'd pull up to her garage, connect to the WiFi, bring up the spreadsheet on the flash drive, email the attachment like she'd taught him, then roll out like Patrick Mahomes on a play action pass. Touchdown; game over. She lived just across the river in the neighboring city and used a different internet provider.

He turned on her street, killed the headlights, paused the music, an pulled up in her driveway with caution. He put the truck in park, powered on the laptop and VOILA, it connected to the WiFi. He did a strong fist pump, "YES," then proceeded to open the file. Still high off the fact that it connected, the garage door began to lift up. He froze as it slowly rose until he was looking in Terrell's eyes.

"What THE..." Terrell began to say, when he saw Deante's truck parked in front of his woman's garage. After hearing her say, "Don't forget the trash people run in the morning, you forgot last week" for what seemed like the 88th time, he decided to take it out, so he could have some peace.

Deante inhaled like Bob Marley in his heyday, "GREAT. Jusssssst GREAT," as he exhaled. He tried to get ahead of the situation as best as possible and diffuse it. "Say mane, it's not what it looks like?

"It's not what it looks like?! It's not what it looks like?! It LOOKS like you're in front of my gal's house with ya laptop out playing with yourself," Terrell rebutted.

"Bruh, it ain't eeen like dat," Deante attempted to assure him. "Look, I just needed to use the WiFi real quick; it's for my job and then I'm leaving. Nothing more, nothing less. Ion want ya girl an she on't want me."

"What I need you to do, is get yo broke a$$ out dis driveway, before I come back, or we gone have a problem," Terrell promised in an eerily calm voice. He left the trash bin where it was, turned around and walked with purpose back towards the house. But not before he could be heard saying, "Now wonder why she left this loser."

"Uh-HA, is that right?" Deante rhetorically asked as he shook his head up and down, "Ok then, COOL" he hit send on the email, closed up the laptop, tossed it to the side, backed out the driveway, then left the way he came. Before he could get to the end of the street, he was already texting. He pulled over, as soon as he got out of the neighborhood, to double check before he hit the white up arrow enclosed in the blue circle.

LaKeisha's phone vibrated and dinged. Terrell looked in its direction, "I KNOW dis fool ain't texting you. I just KNOW dat's not him. Can't be. No Way. Give it here," he politely demanded, with his hand extended. He looked at it, then gave it back to her, "Unlock it." She reluctantly did, then handed it back. They hadn't been messing around or even talking much, so she was certain it wasn't anything incriminating, and surely, he wasn't talking crazy about Tee. "He's probably just apologizing, knowing Deante," she presumed.

"You should be thanking Gawd, that I took you off that free loading bum's hands. You deserve nothing but the best," Terrell said, puffed-up and full of bravado, as he opened the text.

It read: *Since big money grip wanna be the man, and talk all cavalier about me using MY WIFI, he can start paying the bill; along with cellphone and car insurance. I'll be taking your name off of those in the morning as well as cancelling the WiFi. Please make sure to return the equipment. Thank you, take care and be blessed.*

Terrell had no clue that Deante was still paying those bills. It really wasn't a big deal to Deante, since Keisha had been so helpful during and even after their relationship. Plus, she was instrumental in him getting that new promotion. Terrell's stomach started aching. Suddenly he didn't feel so mighty. He handed her phone back and went to the bathroom. He sat on the side of the tub and began reflecting. He'd enjoyed the free WiFi, communicated with her daily on the phone Deante was paying for and even driven the car that he was insuring. Now all of that would fall on him and who knows what else.

Capítulo Diez (Main Condolences)

The harmoniously soothing sounds from the ministers of music, comforted the congregation who listened intently with their ears and heart. The pastor shared his final words, concluding the lovely homegoing celebration. His words and message were just what Bianca needed. With her trying to do all she could to be there for the family, she'd begun to carry too much of a burden herself. Not to mention, she hadn't even scratched the surface in dealing with her own anguish and wounds. Although she and her darling Drew had drifted apart over the last year, she was hopeful that they would eventually mend the fractured relationship and restore it to when it was at its perfected peak.

His mother softly grabbed her by the hand, "Thank you," she emotionally uttered, "for sitting up here. You've always been there for not only my baby Andrew, but also for us." His mom was one of the few individuals who knew and referred to him by his middle name. That's actually where Bianca got it from. She'd overheard his mother calling him that and adopted the beloved moniker for herself. She'd shortened it to Drew, so it could be her own pet name for him.

Bianca didn't quite know what to say, so she simply hugged his mom as an "I love you," lowly flowed outward from her heart. The last year had been nearly unbearable for Bianca. She was fired when new management took over the company she envisioned retiring at, her mother was diagnosed with breast cancer and her child with Drew was stillborn. Since their lost, they'd spoken and spent less and less time together. She knew how much a son would've meant to him. He'd all but completely shut down. They went from Bonnie and Clyde, to never being in the same ride. From spending every major holiday as one, to him doing his own thing with friends. Last Thanksgiving, he went to his aunt's house in Florida without her and then chose to bring in the New Year out of town in Vegas with his boys instead of by her side at watch night. To top it off, on the day she wanted to be there for him the most (Father's Day) he'd left home early and stayed gone the entire time, with his phone off mind you, and when he finally returned, didn't touch any of the food she'd cooked and saved for him. Although they shared the same house, they'd been living in separate realities lately.

Bianca's best friend Jazmine tapped her on the shoulder. "There goes some of his there," she pointed out. Bianca had asked her to be on the lookout for any of his friends. She had decided to make a real effort to check on and be there for everyone he was close to. She felt he would have appreciated and wanted that.

"Ok good good, I'll try to catch them on the way out," she thankfully replied. She'd pointed out a few of his friends in the back, including the girl he'd worked with, whom he said was like a sister to him. And of course, his best friend that she never really cared for. She always felt he was a bad influence on Drew.

They all stood as the funeral director called for the flowers to be collected, while the pallbearers prepared to carry the coffin. "Those are some beautiful flowers," Bianca thought. "Drew would've approved. He used to buy me flowers and compliment the ones I tried to grow in the backyard," she further reminisced.

She and the family followed suit as his casket was being rolled towards the church's exit. As the leaving line came to a halt near the doors, she took advantage of the time by speaking to Drew's work sister who was sitting next to his childhood friend, "You're coming to the repast, right? I know y'all were close and I'd love for all his real friends to be there. I'm sure it'd mean a lot to him," purposely overlooking his closest friend.

After a brief moment of silence, she replied, "We'll see," then confirmed that his boy had the address.

"Cool, looking forward to it," Bianca enthusiastically responded.